Bear's Dream

First published in the UK in 2000 by
Madcap Books
an imprint of André Deutsch Ltd
76 Dean Street
London
W1V 5HA

www.vci.co.uk

Devised and produced by
Tucker Slingsby Ltd,
Berkeley House,
73 Upper Richmond Road,
London SW15 2SZ

1 3 5 7 9 10 8 6 4 2

ISBN 0 233 99764 4

Printed in Singapore by Tien Wah Press (Pty) Ltd

Colour reproduction by Bright Arts Graphics, Singapore

Bear's Dream

Janet Slingsby

Illustrated by Tony Morris

MADCAP

Teddy Bear couldn't get to sleep. 'Humph,' he said crossly and sat up in bed.

By the window a large book lay open on the floor. He slid out of bed and went over to take a look. The book was full of photographs of real bears. There were bears fishing in a river and bears playing in the snow.

'How wonderful to be a wild bear!' thought Teddy Bear. 'I'd like to go wild and have adventures. I'm bored with being a teddy.'

He began to think of running away and what he would need to pack in his rucksack − a clean hankie, a pen to write postcards home, his spectacles...

Splash! A shower of cold, cold water hit Teddy Bear in the face.
'What was that?' he cried.

Whoosh! Wash! More cold water trickled down his fur. Two brown bear cubs were shaking water out of their coats and all over him.

'What sort of wild bears are you?' asked Teddy Bear. 'And why are you so wet?'

'We are grizzly bears,' said one of the cubs. 'We've been helping our mother to catch fish. Come and have a go.'

'This is an adventure,' said Teddy Bear bravely.

The two cubs bounced down to the river and jumped straight in. Their mother stood in the water. She was a very, very big bear with long claws and large teeth. She held a huge, silvery fish in her paw.

'Come and eat some salmon,' cried the cubs.

Teddy Bear thought about cold water, long claws and big teeth. He thought about eating raw, slippery fish...

He waved goodbye to the grizzly bear cubs and trotted away, his rucksack bobbing up and down on his back.

'Mmmm,' Teddy Bear said, feeling the hot sun on his damp fur, 'This looks like the right place to have a dry, warm sort of adventure!'

He stared around at the dry grass and the tall trees. In the distance he saw some animals hopping by.

   'Real kangaroos,' he cried. 'Wait till I tell my friend Hoppy about this!'

The sun beat down.

   'This adventure is getting a bit too warm,' Teddy Bear thought. 'I could do with a cold drink.'

He sat down in the shade of a big tree.

Teddy Bear looked
up and saw something moving
in the tree. He climbed up to see
what it was.

'What sort of wild bear are you?' he
asked the sleepy creature at the top of
the tree.

'I'm not a bear, I'm a koala,' yawned the creature. 'You woke me up. I usually sleep all day and have a good feed in the evening.'

'What do you eat?' said Teddy Bear who was feeling hungry now as well as thirsty.

'Leaves, delicious leaves,' said the koala. 'Try one.'

'Ugh,' choked Teddy Bear. 'I don't think I like these leaves. Can I have a drink please?'

'Oh! I don't drink,' said the koala. 'I only eat leaves.'

'This adventure is not much fun!' said Teddy Bear. 'I am hot, hungry and thirsty.'

So he waved goodbye to the koala and trotted away, wishing he had put some sandwiches and a drink in his rucksack.

Teddy Bear heard a loud slurping, sucking, snuffling sort of sound. 'Perhaps it's someone eating a huge ice cream,' he thought hungrily. He hurried off to look and found a strange bear with his nose in a hole in the ground.

'What sort of wild bear are you?' asked Teddy Bear.
　'I am a sloth bear,' said the bear pulling his nose out.
　'What are you doing?' asked Teddy Bear.
　'I'm sucking up ants and termites,' said the sloth bear.
　'Why?' asked Teddy Bear amazed.
　'To eat them of course,' replied the sloth bear.
　'Oh no,' said Teddy Bear. 'More horrible eating habits!
I am not staying here.'

　So he waved goodbye to the sloth bear and
　　trotted away.

'I thought wild bears ate honey,' said Teddy Bear sadly.

'I do eat honey,' said a loud, growly voice. 'It's my favourite food.'

'What sort of wild bear are you?' asked Teddy Bear.

'I am a sun bear,' said the big bear.

'If you want some honey, jump on my back and hold on tight!'

'This is an adventure,' said Teddy Bear bravely as he clambered on to the sun bear's back.

The sun bear began to climb a very tall tree. He climbed higher and higher.

Teddy Bear shut his eyes. He opened them again when he heard the sound of angry buzzing. The sun bear had his paw inside a bees' nest and angry bees were flying all around them. One large bee stung Teddy Bear on the nose.

'Ouch,' he cried and waved his arms to scare the bees away. Next thing he knew he was falling down and down.

'As far as I am concerned,' said Teddy
Bear, 'honey comes in jars'.
   He was hanging upside down in a big green
bush, his rucksack hooked over a branch. He
rubbed his nose.

'What's honey?' said a voice next to him.

'I know what kind of wild bear you are,' said Teddy Bear. 'You are a panda. You look just like a toy panda I know.'

'I am a panda,' said the baby panda, 'but I am not a bear'.

'What sort of food do you eat?' asked Teddy Bear who thought pandas looked a lot like bears but was too hungry to argue. He hoped pandas ate cake and sandwiches.

'Come and meet my mum,' said the baby panda. 'She will give you some bamboo.'

Teddy Bear was very disappointed to discover that bamboo was a sort of green stick. One shoot was quite enough!

'I am afraid I can't stay,' said Teddy Bear. 'I have to go off in search of more adventures.'

And he waved goodbye and trotted away.

'That bear is wearing glasses,' thought Teddy Bear. 'What sort of wild bear are you?' he asked.

'I am a spectacled bear,' said the strange-looking bear. 'I'm called that because my fur makes me look as if I am wearing glasses.'

The spectacled bear was sitting in a tree, eating fruit. He gave some to Teddy Bear. It was the best wild bear food Teddy Bear had tried.

'I like it here,' said Teddy Bear looking at the mountains in the distance. 'Perhaps I can live like a wild spectacled bear for a few days.' And he began to search in his rucksack for his glasses.

Suddenly, Teddy Bear heard loud shouts. A big clod of earth flew past, just missing his sore nose. 'What's happening?' he cried.

'It's the villagers,' shouted the spectacled bear. 'They don't like us eating the fruit. Run away as fast as you can!' And the spectacled bear rushed away without stopping to say goodbye.

Teddy Bear trotted after him as fast as he could, his rucksack bobbing up and down on his back.

'Now where am I?' said Teddy Bear. 'It's very cold and there's nothing but snow and ice here. No bears at all. What shall I do?'

Then he saw big paw prints in the snow. 'Perhaps they'll lead me to a bear. This is a real adventure,' said Teddy Bear with a shiver, 'but I wish I had packed a jumper'.

Teddy Bear saw a black dot in the distance. He plodded towards it. When he got closer, he saw the black dot was the nose of a huge white bear.

'What sort of wild bear are you?' he asked, feeling a little scared.
   'I'm a polar bear,' she growled. 'Come and meet my cubs.'

Two polar bear cubs were playing in the snow.

'Come and slide on the ice with us,' they cried. 'Let's play snowballs!'

Teddy Bear played in the snow until he was soaked to his stuffing. He was very glad when mother bear said it was time to go home. He was looking forward to drying out in front of a warm fire.

The bears disappeared
down a hole in the snow. Teddy
Bear scurried after them.

'Is this where you live?' he
asked, a little disappointed.

The polar bears' den had no
fire and no furniture. It was just
a hole in the ice.

Teddy Bear curled up between
the sleeping cubs and tried not
to think about his cosy bed at
home. 'This is an adventure!' he
said in a small voice.